ZOMBIE ZERO
THE SHORT STORIES

THE SICKNESS SPREADS

Zombie Zero: The Short Stories
The Sickness Spreads

ISBN-13: 978-1-944916-94-7
ISBN-10: 1-1-944916-94-6

www.SuddenInsightPublishing.com
Indie publishing for the Indie Author

ZOMBIE ZERO
THE SHORT STORIES

THE SICKNESS SPREADS

J.K. NORRY

FOREWORD

This was destined to be the 'Year of the Zombie' for me, and I've embraced that destiny in more ways than anticipated. At first I was going to spend the whole year writing one long book, and release it in time for Halloween. Then the story began to speak to me, and informed me in no uncertain terms that it was going to need more from me. A whole lot more. I had to dedicate myself to writing like never before to pull it off; once I did, it all began to fall into place.

I got a jump on the first book, and started writing it in 2015. It's a good thing I did; like I said, it turned out to just be the first book. It's called 'Zombie Zero: The First Zombie'. If you've read it, I hope you loved it! If not, you can read the prologue for free on my website; it might help flesh out these stories a little better for you (heh, heh; I said flesh). These are some of the stories that wouldn't fit neatly in the book, yet were crying out to be told. I listen closely when a story speaks to me; I can't stand to hear them cry.

There will be six of these smaller books released, each containing a collection of short stories from the world of 'Zombie Zero'. In true short story fashion, each tale stands on its own. So does each book. In keeping with my theme for the year, all of the stories fit together quite nicely as well; they also tie into the books. It doesn't matter where you start, although the books themselves might be better read in order; besides 'Zombie Zero: The First Zombie' and 'Zombie Zero: The Last Zombie', you can be as indiscriminate about reading these stories as a dedicated zombie is to eating folks. If you want to start where I would have you begin, you are in the right place.

There are three stories in this book. Although they weren't the first ones I wrote, it quickly became apparent that it was the first set that we needed to release. Like every story that comes to my inner doorstep, each of these stories is special to me in its own way. They tie in pretty tightly with each other; they also tie in to the events in Chapter eight of 'Zombie Zero: The First Zombie'. You'll soon see why this set is aptly titled 'The Sickness Spreads'.

ABOUT THE SHORT STORIES

First off, let me assure you that there are no spoilers in the following message. The introductions before each story will not contain any information that might give away anything in other stories or the books. I will point out what chapter they tie into, when appropriate, for those that have read 'Zombie Zero: The First Zombie'; but I'll identify it by number, and not give away any critical information. No spoilers; I wouldn't do that to you.

Also, you don't need to read the commentary. For those folks interested in the background of the story and my life in writing this year, it's a little bonus. If you're not that person, I'm not offended; get on to those stories! I hope you love them! Thanks for reading!

Most of these were written on our side porch, on a MacBook Air using Scrivener software. I love the outdoors, and our happy home; it's the perfect mixture of both, a great place to write in sunny California almost year round.

During this project I kept to my writing goals religiously; when I colored outside the lines, it was more often over my daily limit than under. These were very fun to write.

Some of that fun is worth sharing. That's what these sections between stories will be about. As the world of 'Zombie Zero' comes together more fully for you, so will the adventure that it's been writing and publishing all of this. You'll know what order they were written in, find out why I decided to place them in the order they appear here, and what strikes me as special about each story.

When one story spoke to me, I wondered how many others there might be. I thought it would be fun, to have another book to go along with the two that were shaping up. It soon became evident that there were too many short stories for one volume; we bumped it up to three. Finally, the vision stabilized at eighteen short stories spread across six books.

Next, it was time to let the artist speak in his own way. We loved what he did with the first book cover; it inspired us to give him more options when it came time to ask if he would do these covers as well. Let me tell you about that, and about Sean Harrington.

ODE TO SEAN HARRINGTON

Did you see that cover? The one on the first page of the ebook, or the cover of the print book? Look again, if you want; I'll wait, and it's worth it. That art comes from the mind of Sean Harrington, not just from his hands. It's his talent, in part, that made us want to make these collections into six individual books.

I had very specific ideas for the covers of the two companion novels, 'The First Zombie' and 'The Last Zombie'. We found an artist that we liked, and commissioned him to do them. I sent off a detailed description of the first one, crappy sketch attached, and we waited.

It was perfect! It was exactly what I had asked for, with only one minor change. And the really cool thing was that the change was my favorite part! I was elated! I messaged Sean to tell him so; he messaged back to say he was glad I was happy, in a much calmer tone and with way less words. I told him to expect to hear from us in a couple months, for the other cover.

Much discussion ensued, and many short stories. By the time I got back to him, I had a lot more to ask for. Most of all, I wanted him to be a happy artist. So the first thing I did was ask how we could achieve that. I told him about the short stories, and how we'd like him to do those covers too. In the best way I knew how, I asked him how he would like to go about it. Would you like to come up with six concepts for these covers? Would you like to read them, or have me send you synopses? Or do you want me to just tell you what I would think of for them, like I did with the others?

Sean messaged, and said send over some synopses. I was thrilled. It was exciting to wait for the first piece; I had no idea what to expect, except for more great art. Then I saw the first cover, this one, and I was over the moon. It's way better than what I would have come up with. Sean Harrington's concept mind is as phenomenal as his artist's hand, and I couldn't be more grateful to have both at work on these covers.

In case you can't tell, I'm bowing in his direction right now. Have another look at that cover, if you want, before you move on. It's totally worth it.

ODE TO DAWN MARSHALL

Did you notice how I said 'we' a bunch of times while telling you about the books and covers? That's something I can't go without explaining, and expressing some gratitude for. Let me tell you a little about my partner in all things, Dawn Marshall.

Dawn is the one that figured out how to start Sudden Insight Publishing, and did all the work required to make it real. Then she learned all the aspects of actual publishing required to get my books in print and ebook format; then she did it. She's still doing it, too; and she's learning more all the time. It's amazing to have a partner as smart as her, and as dedicated to making my dreams come true as I am.

It was Dawn that figured out how to do the covers I envisioned for the 'Walking Between Worlds' trilogy. She did each one better than I had imagined it. It was her that suggested getting an artist for the 'Zombie Zero' covers, and her that came up with a list of artist names and websites for me to choose from.

She knows my tastes better than I do sometimes; Dawn suspected all along that I would choose the artist that I did, and be very pleased with the results. She was right on both counts, as she so often is.

From my perspective, she does all the hard work. Dawn is kind enough to say that it looks like I do the hard work, from her perspective. I am very lucky to have such an ideal partner, and such a wonderful partnership. When two souls mate, beautiful things can be born; I am blessed to be a part of a truly functional soulmate relationship. Doing all of this on my own would have been difficult to impossible for me, and this would be 'The Decade of the Zombie' instead of 'The Year of the Zombie'.

When I come up with a great idea, Dawn brings it to life. When I come up with a bad idea, she gently steers me or it in the right direction. When I am fresh out of ideas, she is there with great ideas of her own. When I count my blessings, she always comes up first, second and third.

So here I am, bowing in homage yet again. Some folks just deserve it. My 'Awesome Girl' is definitely one of them. Thanks, Dawn, for making my books and dreams a reality at last.

ABOUT CRYSTAL'S COUGH

This is not the first story I started writing. Five other stories were part or all of the way done when I began this one. Some stories I jumped back and forth between, and the first one I started actually got finished eighth. That one will release later; now I want to tell you a little about writing Crystal's story. I started this story sixth, and finished it sixth too. It was clear that this set needed to be released first as soon as I started writing it. The timeline is perfect for anyone who just read or is about to read the first book; also, the title and cover art were well-suited to follow up the initial release. It all just fit.

The reason the first story is 'Crystal's Cough' is because it's the most zombie-free of all the stories. It's only just beginning to go down, and looking out through Crystal's eyes shows us only what she sees. I won't tell you anything else, except a little about the poem she thinks of while reminiscing about her son. I don't identify it in the story, and I won't quote it here for copyright reasons, but it's worth looking up.

Kahlil Gibran (or Khalil, depending where you look) wrote a beautiful book that serves well as a guidebook to living conscientiously. It's called 'The Prophet'. As a young teen, I read it for the first time; what he said about parenting always stuck with me, as did many other passages from the book. I have re-read it many times since, and always found more to think about in its pages.

As an aside, that 'K' in my name stands for 'Kahlil'. The reason I read the book when I was so young was because my parents owned a copy. In my early twenties, I got pretty heavy into philosophy. It was a special joy to find Kahlil Gibran's work highly regarded. I devoured nearly everything else he had written, and he quickly became a favorite among favorites for me. As far as philosophers and authors go, he remains a relevant and important influence. As far as sharing a name with him, because of his work, it is a special honor.

Okay, enough about me. I hope you enjoy 'Crystal's Cough'; it ties in to the events that happen in Chapter 8 of 'Zombie Zero: The First Zombie'. It also ties into the other two stories in this book; but we'll get to that when we get to it.

CRYSTAL'S COUGH

Crystal put her full attention on her breath. If she breathed out too quickly, the air would whoosh out of her lungs in a series of coughs that would end in a fit of choking. If she breathed out too slowly, the breath would come out in sticky short bursts that would also end in coughing and choking. There could be no pause between breaths; her lungs would quiver in the stillness, and she would find herself gasping for air before the inevitable coughing and choking. The same thing would happen if she breathed in too forcefully, or not forcefully enough.

She didn't know what she had come down with. She did know that it had ruined her first trip abroad. What had begun as an exciting journey to the cradle of civilization had ended almost as soon as she had gotten there. One trip to one museum, and Crystal had gone back to her hotel to take a nap. She had laid there for the next several days, delirious with fever and wracked by endless coughing fits. The fever had broken, just in time for her to pack and catch her flight home. The cough still lingered.

Going to a doctor back home was daunting enough; there was no way Crystal was going to check out the emergency room in another country. As far as she knew, they would refuse to discharge her until after her scheduled return trip. Crystal had barely scraped together the money to make the trip; she couldn't afford to buy another ticket, or pay a doctor to tell her that she needed to rest while hospital staff worked round the clock to make sure she couldn't. She would get home to see her son; and if this was it... well, she was ready.

Glad for a window seat, Crystal kept her eyes forward and her breathing calm. If she turned her head too much to the left or right, she would start coughing again. She tried to read the in-flight magazine; tilting her head forward drew a fresh series of hacking from deep within her lungs as well. Gasping, struggling for breath, she stuffed the publication back into the pouch stitched into the seat in front of her.

Crystal tried to ignore the woman sitting to her right; every few moments she would sigh or laugh, or exclaim something under her breath. She had an electronic device on her lap, and was apparently having a very engaging digital exchange with someone. The woman's elbow dug into Crystal's arm every time she made a sound, which was far too often. After battling with her breathing and her irritation for several minutes, Crystal let the coughing come. She positioned her own elbow so each forceful exhalation pressed it into the woman's space and into her body. It was the most satisfying coughing fit she'd had all week.

Watching her breath so closely was a uniquely strange experience for Crystal. Although her fever had broken, the distorting fog of psychedelia still laced her awareness. She had eaten very little in the last few days; combined with her measured breathing, it seemed to be blowing a sublime little bubble around her tortured experience. Crystal had the unique opportunity to look at her old thoughts through this new lens, and over a dozen hours to do it in. If only the woman sitting next to her would shut the hell up, and stop elbowing her.

Breathing in, breathing out, careful and calm, Crystal thought of all the things she would say to her boy if he were sitting with her, and if she could talk without coughing. She was so proud of him, she had to ask herself why she didn't say so more often.

There in the quiet stark honesty of her mind, she looked more closely at her own feelings.

It had been hard to raise him alone, although not as hard as tolerating his father had been. The greatest difficulty had been Steven's lack of difficulty. He had excelled in school, had put together a healthy and active social life, and participated in after school activities regularly since learning what they were. Steven had been advanced twice, and her greatest fear had been seeing him have difficulty at a higher level of learning and socialization. Each time he had embraced the experience, and made a new circle of friends while somehow keeping in touch with the old ones.

Steven had been a fourteen-year-old high school sophomore when Crystal had gotten a full picture of what was going on. She had attended one of his basketball games, between shifts, without telling him. Usually they rode to and from the games she could attend together; he always walked in with her, and changed quickly after so as not to leave her waiting in the car.

This time she watched him after, interacting with teammates and spectators. He held court on the court, as a stream of kids of all ages came to congratulate him on the game. Crystal watched beefy boys that looked like they would be more comfortable on a wrestling mat or football field come up to embrace him, or shake his hand. She saw boys and girls that looked like they belonged on a street corner smoking something treat Steven with the same respect; she watched pretty girls that looked like they should have been waving pompoms approach him, and several that actually held the colorful streamers in their hands as they hugged him.

Watching, Crystal had realized that a throng of people had formed around him. She also realized that if he saw her, he would break away to come talk to her. Crystal had fought back tears as she watched from the stands; it wasn't just that he was popular, or well-loved. It was the calm grace with which he handled his popularity, the memory of him waving to her in the stands whenever he knew she was there. Thinking back over her own high school persona, in this very same institution, had sent her slinking out the door without being seen.

She wished she had taken the opportunity then, breaking through the crowd to see him see her see him in his element. The only thing Crystal would let matter was that another chance might come, and that she might take it. Controlling her breath helped control her thoughts, and she calmly directed them to paint a picture for her. It was her simple sublime wish come true, putting her arms around Steven and telling him that he had broken her proud meter long ago. With few accomplishments behind her that didn't feel like they had wrung her dry or left her broken, his young ambition had surpassed her own at his first taste of adulthood. Crystal didn't want to tell him that she was proud of him; she wanted to tell him that she was awed by him.

"Can I get you something to drink, ma'am?"

The voice shattered her reverie, and Crystal nearly burst forth with a fresh series of wet hacking. A quick sideways glance told her that the flight attendant was addressing the woman to her right; Crystal had a few moments to gather her thoughts and her wind while she readied her own response. She knew a glass of water or something with bubbles in it would soothe her throat if it was cold; even just sucking a piece of ice would help her keep things clear. At the thought, a thirst started in her belly to climb scratching tendrils up her esophagus. The picture formed in her mind just as a fit of coughing sent her gasping for air.

While Crystal struggled and choked, the woman to her right gave her drink order. She gave Crystal a hateful glance, and asked for a double. Crystal's only drink order was pained gasping, coughing and choking; she tried to make the shape of a bottle of water, or share the image of it in her mind with the woman; but the coughing threw her fingers spastically out of configuration. The flight attendant gave up at the same time as she did, and Crystal went back to her breathing while the woman moved on to the next aisle.

She thought again of Steven, of his scholarship and his upcoming graduation. Crystal knew he wanted her there, and nothing would please her more than to make it that long; yet a part of her couldn't help imagining the event without her, and the rest of his life after that. She had never been much for poetry; but she had always carried one line from one poem in her heart, as far back as she could remember. It was a reminder from a poet philosopher to parents, that their children did not belong to them. Crystal had first read it when she was very young, and the chord it struck within her had helped her find her independence and her strength. No matter how her parents had battered her after that, the phrase had been a shield their blows could never fully penetrate.

It had been liberating when she was dependent on them, to think that she came through her parents rather than from them. When she had become a young mother, Crystal had used the simple guideline in every way she could apply it in raising up Steven. The struggles of every other area of life had not foreshadowed the joys of motherhood for her in any way, and she had taken to it like a fish to water. Suddenly her life had had purpose; it was as if Crystal had been dropped into the timeline of her own life with another person's wisdom. In realizing she was but an instrument of propulsion for Steven, Crystal had shaped herself to be the best bow that she could be. Watching her son shoot forth straight and true like a finely crafted arrow felt as effortless to her as feeling her heart swell with love at the sight of him.

She felt a twisting whirl of pain in her belly, as if her flesh was swirling with a thousand tiny tendrils all traveling in a narrowing circle. The prickling sensation crawled just under the surface of her skin as it spiraled toward her belly button.

Crystal felt a painful wrenching as they came together as one sharp sensation, and she started coughing uncontrollably once more. The flight attendant returned while she was gasping for air, and Crystal watched enviously as the woman next to her sipped at her bubbly drink before setting it down.

It was no more in her to steal than it was to murder; Crystal watched her own hand with horror as it reached out on its own, as if it were committing one and not the other. When the cup moved to her lips, she couldn't help but sip at it; setting it down, she gasped at the stark flavor as the cool wet coated her throat with momentary numbness. It wasn't enough to wash away the scratching, or numb her throat to the point of painlessness; but it was something. For several minutes Crystal was able to sit and breathe normally.

It seemed that taking all that time to breathe in a controlled fashion and having a good look at her thoughts had calmed her considerably. Typically she lay in bed for a good long while before falling asleep, and dozing while sitting up in a public place was beyond her imagining. Now she felt calm, relaxed and on the verge of drifting off. Of course, a handful of restless nights wrapped in blankets stained by her own fevered sweat was probably contributing to the equation considerably; and the unfamiliar flavor of whiskey still lingered in the back of her raw and ragged throat, pressing her closer to the brink of unconsciousness. Crystal saw it coming, and opened her arms to it. Nothing would be better than sleeping away the rest of the flight.

"Oh my gosh!" The woman to her right cried out, elbowing Crystal as she did. She was torn from the brink of sweet restful unconsciousness to the harsh reality of people's general lack of consideration. A fresh spasm passed over her lungs, and a loud series of coughs erupted from her mouth. Crystal made a gargantuan effort to get her breathing back under control, trying not to curse the woman typing on her electronic device. The woman turned her head and leaned to look at the woman seated on her other side, as Crystal wished the kindest thoughts she could at her, and Crystal took it as a sign. She drained the woman's drink.

The woman bumped her with an elbow as she lifted her hand to press the call button. She bumped her again, on the way down, and Crystal breathed with the detached regularity of a monk during meditation as she did. The only sound in her mind was a calm voice, counting the offenses; it was how many sips she would allow herself from the woman's beverage, should opportunity arise. Rather than dread the inevitable offenses, Crystal looked forward to tallying them as they came.

By the time the woman fell asleep beside her, Crystal had drunk the lion's share of three whiskey and sodas. She would have never thought to request the bitter bubbles for herself, but it seemed to be just what the doctor ordered. The woman bought a fourth drink before she nodded off, and only took a couple sips before closing her eyes. When she began to snore lightly, Crystal sipped at the drink as if it were her own. Soon she had a nice buzz, and her own eyelids grew heavy once more. Balling up her jacket and stuffing it between the window and her seat's headrest, Crystal leaned her head into the ball and closed her eyes.

*   *   *

Waking up was not the easy startling snap that she was used to. Crystal found herself in darkness, staring up at a distant pinpoint of light. It seemed very far away, and drifting further as she watched it. Somehow she knew that was the path, the portal she must pass through to gain control of her own body once again. It seemed so far, and she was only pushing it further away with her efforts to grasp at it. It was as though her body was taking control of itself, squeezing her out until her entire experience was confined to her darkest depths.

She may have given into the darkness, on any other day. Crystal had learned long ago that her attempts at tugging on her own bootstraps generally ended up with her on her ass. She had always wondered how such a phrase could make sense, in a world so obviously governed by the laws of physics. Santa Claus and the Easter Bunny had been replaced by much more nefarious stories as she got older, and Crystal had believed the lies that adults tell adults as easily as she had believed the lies adults tell children. The only people she had seen lift themselves up by their own bootstraps were comic book and movie superheroes. Crystal could no more fly to that pinpoint of light than she could rise above her own limitations. The thought of Steven was enough to keep it shining, like a distant star; but nothing she did brought it any closer.

Watching it, she realized that she was no

longer asleep. Her eyes were open: that was the distant speck of light, the view through her own eyes. Behind her eyes, between her and that view, it was not just darkness. It was a palpable darkness, a shade of inky black with a consciousness of its own. She felt it in the cloud of drifting shadows, thoughts and needs all subjugated to a strange twisting hunger. It was like waking up and realizing she was not in bed alone, and that the stranger next to her was an uninvited and unexpected intruder. It was no tangle of blankets next to her, nor a vast emptiness above her. There was something between her and her own eyes, something more than empty space. Crystal didn't have to fly; she could climb.

It seemed to feel her, to try and shake her off. Crystal clung to it, grabbed at it, pulled herself over it and through it. She came conscious with the sudden sound of a loud bubble popping, and her senses were her own again. It was almost too much, sights and sounds and smells clambering at her all at once. She looked at the woman seated next to her. For a moment her ashen face and sunken cheeks made Crystal wonder if she was dead. Looking past her, at the next passenger over, she wondered if maybe everyone on the flight was dead. The woman next to her took a long breath in her sleep, and shifted slightly. Crystal shook off the feeling, and the last vestiges of drunkenness, just as the captain announced that they would be landing soon. She watched the woman next to her come awake, and try to take a drink; she looked puzzled as she took the empty cup from her lips and stared sleepily at it.

Crystal felt a wave of guilt wash over her. She opened her mouth, to apologize, to explain; she spewed spittle all over the seat in front of her as she coughed uncontrollably instead. The woman turned further from her, and ignored her until she shuffled out with the other passengers. She saw her again at baggage claim, and the woman looked awful. Her shoulders sagged, her eyes were dark sunken hollows, and her grayed skin appeared to be barely clinging to her face. It looked like she was coming toward her for a moment; Crystal saw the woman look her way, and start moving forward; then the view was blocked by a man and a woman as they stepped before her.

They were dressed nearly identically, in dark pressed suits over stark starched white shirts. He wore a dark colored tie; she wore a light scarf.

"Excuse me, ma'am," the man said. "We're going to have to ask you to come with us."

They looked poised to prevent her escape, perhaps prepared to draw weapons. Crystal laughed, which led to a brief coughing fit, then laughed again.

"I'm sorry," she said. "You must have me confused with someone else."

They exchanged a puzzled glance, as if her lucidity surprised them; nonetheless, the man shook his head firmly.

"Please," he repeated. "Come with us."

She moved in the direction they indicated, and they followed. The man spoke again while they walked, from behind her.

"We need to ask you some questions," he said, "about the people sitting near you on your flight."

Crystal glanced back over her shoulder.

"There's the woman that was sitting next to me," she nodded. "I don't see the young lady that was on the other side of her. Those are the only people I really made any note of. Sorry."

"That's fine," the woman responded. They came to a door marked 'Security Personnel Only'; the man punched a code into the keypad, and opened the door for them. The woman ushered Crystal into the room beyond. Crystal took a few steps; she stopped, tried to turn as the door clicked shut. There was a small cell in the corner of the room, big enough for a person to stand or sit without being so large as to actually afford occupants any actual comfort. When she saw it Crystal turned instinctively away from the cage; she bumped into the man as he came up behind her.

"What is this all about?" Crystal asked. Her voice was trembling.

The man glanced at the cell. "Ma'am, we believe you have been exposed to a virus that could very well cause an outbreak. We need to take you into custody, for your safety and the safety of others."

"I...I would never hurt anyone," Crystal squeaked.

"Of course," the man smiled. "Nonetheless, we need you to wait in the cell. It won't be long. We just need to get the other woman you pointed out before she has a chance to get away."

Crystal eyed the grated metal, glanced at the woman. Her eyes were as cold and flat as her suit; she nodded toward the cage. It was not the first time that Crystal had realized that even a true democracy only worked out for the privileged majority. She stepped into the containment unit, heard the lock click as the door shut behind her. By the time she had wiped her tears, and turned, she was alone in the room.

* * *

They put her in a room all by herself at the hospital. She could see that there was someone in the room next to her, separated only by translucent plastic curtains; but the presence was no comfort. Crystal heard her through the plastic, moaning and growling and mewling. She could tell it was a female, but she could also tell that those were not words in any language. The woman's voice was that of a hungry animal, or a tortured one. People came in to bring Crystal food and drink; no one visited the woman in the next room.

Every time a nurse or doctor or aide would come in, they wore suits and masks that made it feel like they weren't really quite in the room with her. Each visit she cried out her son's name, called out his phone number; they had taken her clothes and her things, and Crystal had nothing left but the mercy of others. For two days she laid there, listening to the woman moan through thick sheets of plastic and watching the latest unbelievable international news story unfold on the television they had provided her. Her cough seemed to have gotten a little better, but she dared not sleep; something awaited her in her slumber, something that did not ever want her to wake up again. Her mind became numb and scattered as time passed, and soon she couldn't seem to tell what pictures on the screen were fiction and which were news reports. It seemed like every channel was showing monster movies round the clock.

Crystal almost didn't recognize Steven when he came in; her mind was ravaged by the virus and the struggle to stay awake. His face was hidden behind a clear view screen, his familiar body language masked by the bulky quarantine suit. It wasn't until she heard his voice that Crystal sat up, and reached for him.

"Mama?" he murmured, quietly.

Crystal nodded, smiled, opened her arms to him. Steven rushed to her side, wrapped her in cold plastic. He held her tight, and Crystal let herself cry all the tears she had kept inside while he did. Steven made no move to let her go until she did, and Crystal looked up at him as he drew away.

Wiping away her tears, smiling through the fog, Crystal tried to choose words. He was so handsome, but she didn't need to tell him that; he was such a good boy, but that just sounded demeaning. He hadn't grown completely into manhood yet, but she knew it would suit him like everything else; she also knew that she was not going to see it. From the moment the fever had first taken her, days ago, Crystal had entertained the notion almost constantly that this would be her final challenge. Whatever had climbed inside of her lungs and her belly was going to win the battle she was fighting eventually. As the days wore on, even after the fever had broken, the thought had come to her again and again: she wasn't going to beat this.

It only took one look at Steven to confirm that he saw the same reality through his bright youthful eyes that she was seeing through her old dull ones, for once. She patted his arm though the plastic sleeve, and nodded.

"I admire you, Steven," Crystal said quietly. "It's not normal maybe for a mother to admire her child, but I don't care. It's not why I admire you. I got to know you because I got to give birth to you, and I feel so blessed because of both. I wouldn't have gotten to know you any other way, and my heart would not have been changed forever by you."

Crystal started coughing, and Steven tried to shush her; but she waved him off, and clutched his gloved hand.

"No, listen," she sputtered. Crystal cleared her throat, went on. "I didn't have a chance to watch you do all the things you're going to do. If the folks in charge on the other side let me, though, you can bet I'll see it all. Don't you worry about falling down, or messing up; you just remember I'm still praying for you, and tugging on the Lord's sleeve every time I get a chance. And all the rest of the time, when you stand tall and proud and victorious, don't you ever wish your mama was there to see it. I'll be there. I'll see it. I'll be in awe of you, even after..."

She didn't want to finish the sentence, and he didn't want to finish it for her. They sat in silence, holding hands, until another figure shrouded in plastic stepped into the room. He looked at Steven.

"Five more minutes," his muffled voice pronounced.

"Are these restraints really necessary?"

Steven called out, pulling at the thick fabric holding one of Crystal's wrists at her side.

She patted Steven's hand, reassuringly.

"It's okay," she murmured. "I don't need to go anywhere. All I need is right here. I know it's over."

Steven exchanged a look with the man through their visors; the stranger moved closer, and Crystal recognized him. She saw the collar of his black suit through the transparent pane, and his partner came in behind him. She moved with him to the side of Crystal's bed, and she was suddenly surrounded by three clunky quarantine outfits.

"What do you mean?" The man looked down at her curiously.

Crystal coughed, glanced at each of them in turn. She lowered her eyes guiltily.

"I know I caught something over there," she admitted. "I knew it when I was there, but I wanted to get home. I didn't mean to hurt anyone, or put anyone in any kind of danger. I just wanted to see my son. Please tell me that no one else got sick."

Steven glanced at the television for some reason. It was muted, playing yet another in an endless stream of monster movies. He let go her hand, stood and walked over to shut it off. Standing at her side once more, he took her hand in both of his.

The pair that had brought her here exchanged a look. She shrugged, and he began speaking.

"Ma'am, you just had a cold or a flu," he said. "That is not why you are here. You are here because you sat next to-"

"Agent," Steven cut him off. "Is this really the time for a world news update?" He looked pointedly down at his mother.

Crystal felt a sharp pang of anxiety twist her belly. She looked up at Steven, then at the man he had interrupted. Her confused eyes found the woman last; she looked away.

"What are you talking about?" Crystal whispered.

Steven smiled, leaned in closer to her.

"Mama," he said, "the nice man is trying to tell you that you didn't do anything wrong. You didn't get anyone sick, and you didn't hurt anyone. He just feels awkward because your condition is terminal."

Crystal coughed, looked at the man hopefully.

"Isn't that right, Agent?" Steven asked.

"Of course." The man nodded. "I'm so sorry, ma'am. You aren't going to make it. But you didn't get anyone sick. In fact, you helped us get research we may need to..."

He trailed off, glanced at Steven.

"You helped us fight other such conditions in future scenarios," he finished. Steven was nodding as Crystal's eyes found his.

"You helped, Mama," he said. "You saved me, too. These nice folks are going to help me, and make sure I don't have any chance of getting sick. Because of what you did."

Crystal was confused again. She looked back and forth between her visitors, her brow knitted.

"We need to go," the woman said. "We still need to try to talk to the other one."

The man nodded, reached out his gloved hand over Crystal's body. Steven grasped it, shook it.

"Get somewhere safe," the man said.

Steven nodded. "I will. Thank you."

He glanced at his mother. "For everything."

Crystal felt him squeeze her hand; it was a distant sensation, as if she were the one coated in thick plastic. She felt something clawing at her from within, that final sleep that she had been avoiding so fervently. The touch of his hand made Crystal realize that she didn't need to run any more. She was ready for the next world. She tried to squeeze his hand back, found that she couldn't. Crystal watched him through hazy confusion as Steven leaned over her one last time.

"It's okay, Mama," he said. There were tears on his visor. "I'll be okay. You can let go. You can go home if you want to."

She smiled, or she tried to. Instead her eyes closed, and Crystal marveled at the singular sound of her heart monitor as it slowed. There was a weak beep, and another; then the noise settled into one long lazy beep that would not end until someone came along to shut off the machine. Steven let go of her hand, and slipped out of the room.

ABOUT BARBARA'S TRIP

I hope you liked 'Crystal's Cough'. That was kind of sweet, wasn't it? And no zombies, really. Just the threat spreading all around her...

Speaking of sweet...

Remember the woman on the plane next to Crystal, the one who was bothering her so much? Well, her name is Barbara. She's actually a really nice lady. Her work ethic and goal-setting and her real love for her husband appealed to me; when I saw how she saw things, I knew Barbara's story had to be told. To someone, she's the most considerate person in the world.

I've always been fascinated by differences in perspectives. I realized a long time ago that most people see themselves as the protagonist in their own story. Some people see themselves as near saintly, even. Very few people see themselves as a villain, no matter how monstrously they treat others. I think it's important to realize that we only stay alive by eating life; just like zombies, we are bound to kill by our own need to feed.

From some perspective, we're all monsters. You should see me in the garden! I'll stand there right in the middle of everything, let plants watch while I bite into what used to be their neighbor; it's downright savage.

We're ramping things up with this story, but only by a couple notches. That's why it comes after Crystal's, although that's not the order I wrote them in. This one was started and finished fifth, before the one you just read. When I saw the slow build that was happening if the stories were placed in this order, I knew it was the right fit. Things get a little more twisted, and it's clearly going down at this point...but it's not quite time for full-on zombie action.

Don't worry, I won't leave you hanging. There is one more story after this one; if gore is what you're here for, it will be worth the wait. Now, please enjoy 'Barbara's Trip'. This is a slightly stronger tie-in to the events that take place in Chapter 8 of 'Zombie Zero: The First Zombie'. She is, after all, sitting closer to the young woman that Chapter 8 is about; right next to her, actually.

Gross, huh?

BARBARA'S TRIP

The crowded metal tube seemed more crowded than she was used to. Barbara realized that was impossible, of course. A full flight is a full flight, and most of the planes she regularly rode were often full. It was the only thing she hated about traveling for work: airplanes packed full of people. Barbara waited until they had taken off, and the wi-fi indicator came on overhead, sitting patiently and smiling vaguely at nothing. The moment she saw the light come on, she moved to illuminate her device. There was already a message waiting, and a flashing icon. She clicked on it.

ST: 'I miss you so much.'

Barbara frowned, tapped furiously at the screen. She hit send.

BT: 'Don't say that. You know it only makes it harder for me. I won't be home for hours.'

She paused, watching the spinning symbol that indicated a response in progress.

ST: 'I didn't say it. I wrote it.'

"Hah," Barbara muttered humorlessly.

She scowled while she tapped at the screen. She sent the message, and the words appeared under his.

BT: 'Very funny, smart guy. I'm glad to see that your sense of humor has not been affected by your flu.'

She waited.

ST: 'No you're not. If there were a disease that eliminated a person's sense of humor you would take me to an infected neighborhood immediately.'

She laughed out loud, bumping the woman next to her with her elbow. Barbara glanced at her to apologize. The words caught in her throat, and she put her eyes back on the screen. She continued to type after sending the first message, and the two appeared one after the other on the screen.

BT: 'I wouldn't take you; I would send you. I don't want to lose my sense of humor too...I'm actually funny.'

BT: 'Guess who I'm sitting next to.'

Barbara bit her lip while she watched the icon twirl. Without moving her head, she shifted her eyes as far as possible in the young woman's direction. A new batch of characters appeared, and her eyes caught the motion.

ST: 'The President?'

Her fingers were a flurried blur, as Barbara shook her head.

BT: 'Right. The most powerful person in the world decided to forego private jet travel to sit next to me in coach on a sixteen hour flight.'

ST: 'You said guess.'

Barbara typed her response, sent the message with a flourish.

BT: 'You're such a pain in the ass sometimes.'

She giggled.

ST: 'So...who are you sitting next to?'

Biting her lip once more, Barbara flushed while she typed her response. She knew the woman could look over at any time and read what she was writing.

BT: 'A woman with some kind of flesh eating virus or something. It's super icky, and kind of sad. It looks like she was really pretty before her face started to fall off.'

While she watched the icon spin, Barbara was suddenly elbowed repeatedly by the older woman sitting next to her. She was having a coughing fit; every time she hacked loudly, her elbow drove itself into Barbara's ribs. Barbara cleared her throat loudly as a new message appeared on the screen, and the woman apologized between wheezing gasps.

ST: 'Gross. You're so mean sometimes.'

Barbara glanced unabashedly both to her left and right as she readied her response, as if challenging the women she was writing about to read her words.

BT: 'You have no idea what I have to put up with out here. I literally just watched a piece of flesh fall from that girl's face. It's still sitting there in her lap; it's disgusting. The woman on the other side of me is hacking and coughing like crazy, and she keeps elbowing me. If either one of these women are contagious, I could be dead before I ever make it home.'

It was all still on the screen, the things she had written about both women. Barbara leaned back a little in her seat, to give them ample opportunity to pry if they wanted to. Neither of them seemed to notice; the young woman continued to stare straight ahead at nothing; the other started on a fresh coughing fit, spewing spit and phlegm and elbows in every direction.

ST: 'Don't say that.)-:'

Barbara huffed loudly, started typing. His next message showed up before she had finished.

ST: 'Besides, you never get sick.'

Barbara deleted what she had written, started over. She hit send.

BT: 'Some of us don't have time to get sick. Some of us don't get nine paid sick days every year.'

She waited, still wondering if either woman would look over before her words about them scrolled off the top of the lighted screen.

ST: 'Ten, actually. All of which are being used up by this stupid flu.'

Giggling, Barbara composed her next message. She sent it, imagining his reaction as she did. Her giggling became a strangled snort.

BT: 'Aw, poor baby. No fishing trips at the end of the year.'

She watched the last incriminating evidence disappear forever as his reply came through.

ST: 'Yeah, right. I still have vacation time.'

Barbara fumed as she stabbed at the screen. Still fuming, she tapped the send button.

BT: 'No you don't. My parents are coming out this year, remember?'

Barbara cringed away from the young woman falling apart at her right, only to be jabbed in the ribs as the woman on her left burst into a fresh fit of coughing.

ST: 'That's only half my vacation.'

Shaking her head, Barbara hoped he could feel the frown on her face as she composed her rapid-fire messages.

BT: 'The other half is for the tropical getaway you promised me.'

BT: 'Remember?'

Barbara glanced down at her leg, horrified. A tiny piece of flesh was sticking to her pants. It wasn't gooey, or wet; in fact, it looked like it would dry up and flake off if she left it there. She set the device aside, leaned forward and removed the in-flight magazine from the back of the seat in front of her. Grimacing, looking right at the young woman as she continued to visibly deteriorate beside her, Barbara swept the clinging cells from her leg with the magazine. The young woman stared straight ahead; she was lost in her own thoughts, too self-absorbed to notice. Barbara looked back at the screen.

ST: 'Come on, Barbie...can't we do it next year?'

Barbara let out a little yelp, and typed.

BT: 'You know I hate it when you call me that. Another year? Are you kidding me?'

"Can I get you something to drink, ma'am?"

The voice shattered her tenuous link with Stanley; Barbara looked up at the woman. She gave her fellow passengers a deliberate long look, and returned her eyes to the attendant. The woman smiled, a fake plastic smile that did not acknowledge the state of either of the women beside Barbara. The woman to her left began coughing violently; the attendant kept smiling, and staring.

"I'll take a whiskey and soda," Barbara said, frowning at the flight attendant. She waited for the woman to her left to wind down to a wheezing series of quiet gasps for air. "Make it a double, please."

"Ma'am?" The attendant moved her gaze to the wheezing woman. "Anything to drink?"

She waved her hands before her, trying to hold in another round of explosive coughs. After a moment of perhaps trying to speak, or sign, the woman shook her head. As the flight attendant's eyes moved to the woman at Barbara's right, they widened; she drew back a little.

"Ma'am?" she said. Her smile was gone. "Anything to drink?"

The young woman was oblivious, clearly

lost in some inner vision or thought. Barbara looked back and forth between her and the flight attendant, frowning. She raised her eyebrows expectantly, thinking strong drink thoughts forcefully at the woman. Finally, the flight attendant stopped waiting and moved on. Barbara returned her eyes to the screen.

ST: 'Come on, sweetheart. You know I need my fishing trips. You travel all the time. Why not just have a staycation this year?'

Barbara harrumphed loudly, and stabbed at the screen.

BT: 'Because I had a staycation last year. I cleaned out the garage, got caught up on housework and laundry, and didn't relax at all. I can't relax at home; you know that. There's too much to do.'

She frowned while she waited.

ST: 'The garage could always use another cleaning...'

"Oh my gosh!" Barbara blurted loudly, shaking her head. She bent forward, attacked the screen with her fingertips. It was all she could do to ignore the woman coughing loudly to her left.

BT: 'There's that sense of humor again.'

The response was almost immediate.

ST: 'You love it.'

Biting her lip, Barbara leaned into the device once more.

"Ma'am? Your whiskey and soda."

The flight attendant was back, leaning over the woman still falling apart in the aisle seat. Barbara grasped the drink, sipping at it before lowering her beverage tray and setting it down. She dug in her purse for her wallet, paid the woman in cash. There was another message waiting when she returned her eyes to the lighted screen.

ST: 'Right back; feeling queasy.'

Barbara smiled while she sipped her drink. She loved the fact that he didn't abbreviate or misspell words when they messaged each other. They had both commented on how nice it was from the start, to get texts and emails that didn't make either of them feel like they were communicating with a remedial reading student. Their messages were fun, and silly even; but neither of them was apt to make a spelling error. Other than that they could write anything to each other; there were never any hurt feelings, or improperly assigned intonations. The words on the screen were their constant connection; neither of them would violate that, with grudges or bad grammar. Barbara adored the fact that he would rather hold a mouthful of vomit for an extra moment than indulge in the Orwellian newspeak that others seemed to favor when texting her.

The icon was spinning; he was writing.

ST: 'I just totally got sick. Bleh.'

Barbara sipped her drink, typed with one hand.

BT: 'Did you make it to the bathroom?'

Tilting the cup until ice avalanched onto her face, Barbara realized that her cocktail was nearly empty. She tried to lean over the woman in the aisle seat; the pile of flesh that had accumulated on the young lady's lap deterred her. Barbara felt the drink try to come up as she drew back. Her stomach wound itself suddenly into a twisted knot, and icy fingers climbed her spine. She reached up to press the button that would call the flight attendant; her own hand before her face was blurred.

Barbara rubbed her eyes, drew her hand away; it was covered in sweat. Blinking away her blurred vision, she read his next message.

ST: 'Don't worry. I didn't throw up on your precious couch or carpeting. I feel really lousy, by the way. Not that you care.'

"Aww," Barbara murmured under her breath. She typed for a full minute, swallowing down her own queasiness.

BT: 'Of course I care. I think I'm coming down with something too.'

Barbara tilted her cup, carefully, and let one ice cube between her lips. She swirled it in her mouth, holding the melting water in the back of her throat. The itchy feeling at the base of her tongue continued, so she tilted her head back and gargled quietly with the cold whiskey water.

"Ma'am? Can I help you?" The flight attendant was leaning over her suddenly, turning off the call signal as she did.

She started, nearly choking. Barbara swallowed and nodded.

"Could I get another whiskey and soda please?" She held up her empty cup, fought the sudden urge to cough.

The flight attendant looked down at the young woman between them. Her face twisted in disgust, and she met Barbara's eyes before her automated smile replaced the startled expression. Barbara nodded when their gazes met, pointed at the empty cup.

"Another double please?" she said, glancing at the young woman's increasingly horrific face.

"Of course." The flight attendant put her attention on the woman near the window.

"Can I get you anything?"

Barbara hadn't even realized the older woman had stopped coughing until she started up again. It was as if the flight attendant's words were the trigger to her next series of explosions, and as if the woman had been saving them up for several minutes to let them all loose in one endless volley. The attendant waited for several seconds, until it was clear that the woman was not going to respond with anything but wheezing sprays of spittle. Barbara looked back to the lighted screen on her lap.

ST: 'Not allowed. Only one of us can be sick at a time, remember? I'm pretty sure that was in the marriage contract. You signed; it's binding. Sorry, sweetheart. You're going to have to wait your turn.'

Her stomach turned again, and a bead of sweat dripped into one of Barbara's eyes. She wiped her brow with the back of her hand, tapped the screen with the other. When her hand came away from her forehead, it was covered in perspiration. She hit send.

BT: 'It's totally all of the sudden. My throat feels raw and scratchy, I keep getting cold chills, I'm sweaty. I feel like I'm going to throw up too.'

This time she was watching for the flight

attendant, and her drink. Barbara raised her hand over the young woman's head to take it, swallowing the urge to vomit as she imagined a hunk of flesh falling in her cocktail. Pressing bills into the attendant's hand, she nodded when the woman counted the extra cash. She smiled in a way that she hoped would cause her to return soon, and often. Barbara sipped her drink, read his next message.

ST: 'I'm so sorry, baby. I hope you didn't pick up some exotic disease abroad.'

A sudden cough from her own mouth startled her, and Barbara felt thick whiskey-flavored phlegm fluid rush up her throat to fill her mouth. She swallowed, closing her eyes and frowning deeply; then she drained half her cocktail in one drink. The next message was written with a fresh sheen of sweat on the back of her hand and the sour taste of bile in her mouth. She sent it, the shadow of a frown still creasing her face.

BT: 'I get all my shots. More likely it was you, or one of the women sitting next to me. They both look way worse than I feel. Which is saying a lot.'

Barbara glanced at the women; they were each caught up in their own struggle. One was trying to breathe without exploding, and the other seemed to be simply waiting to fall apart completely. She cleared her throat, looked down at his reply.

ST: 'It wasn't me. The doctor said the only time I was contagious was during the week you were in London. Blame one of the ladies.'

Sighing, she typed her response. Barbara had another sip of her drink before she hit send.

BT: 'It doesn't matter where I got it from. You're totally right; I can't get sick right now. I have to be in Australia next week. My schedule is too tight for me to lay around on the couch for two weeks.'

She sipped at her drink again, and got another face full of ice. Barbara held the drink up in disbelief, shook her head, and set it down. She pushed the call button. Stanley's message appeared on the screen.

ST: 'So now you're more important than me? Ouch.'

Barbara snorted derisively, reached a trembling hand to stab at the call button again; glancing up, she realized the indicator light was already glowing. She leaned into the screen as she typed.

BT: 'There are many benefits to being an independent contractor. Thinking that you're the most important person in any situation is seldom one of them. I can't take time off because my customers will find someone else. I don't see how that makes me important in any way.'

He wrote back quickly.

ST: 'You're important to me.'

"Aww," Barbara muttered under her breath. She watched the icon twirl, waited for more.

ST: 'You're the most important thing in the world to me.'

"Mmm-hmmm," she murmured, typing.

"Ma'am?" The flight attendant was back. "Another drink?"

Barbara looked up at her, smiled sweetly. "Could I please?"

"Of course." The woman took her cup full of ice and made her way up the aisle. Barbara finished her message, hit send.

BT: 'And you're the most important thing in the world to me. The harder I work now, the more time we have together later. I'm so happy that we are retiring early instead of having kids. I so look forward to being young and healthy and together all the time with you.'

She imagined it as he composed his response, long walks and long drives and long conversations. There was nothing short about their future together in her mind, including the few years it would take to get there.

ST: 'Me too. I adore you, Barbara.'

"Aww," she said again. She glanced at the women to her left and right. The one on her right was still oblivious to everything but whatever she was thinking about. Barbara stared at her unabashedly for a minute, wondering if her thoughts were as twisted as her features. She saw the flight attendant coming up the aisle with her drink, and sighed in relief. Setting the device aside, she dug in her purse for bills. Barbara had learned long ago that American cash was recognized nearly everywhere. Some folks looked down on a single dollar, but plenty of them lit up at the sight of one. She always kept a wad of them in her purse. As far as she was concerned, the flight attendant could have them all if she just kept bringing her drinks.

She sipped at it while she typed. Her expressions mirrored her message: first she was smiling, as the whiskey flavor completely overwhelmed the taste of bile in her throat; then her belly rumbled and tumbled, and a deep frown creased Barbara's pretty face.

She hit send as an uncomfortable bubble rose slowly along the length of her esophagus.

BT: 'You're so sweet. I adore you as well, darling. Be right back; also not feeling so great.'

Setting the device and her drink near the edge of the tray, Barbara looked at the woman in the aisle seat once more. As much as she loathed the thought of any kind of actual contact with her, she squeezed past. It was all she could do to mutter "excuse me" without having the words come out riding a wave of vomit. As soon as she made it to the bathroom the rising bubble burst within her, and the feeling subsided.

Barbara washed her face with cold water, emptied her bladder, washed her face again, and made her way back to her seat. Eyeing the lighted screen, she noticed with disappointment that the battery life indicator was flashing. She lifted her drink to her lips, and got only ice. Biting her lip in frustration, she began composing a message. A fresh sheen of sweat appeared on her forehead by the time she had slowly selected the characters that would construct the first sentence. Reaching through the murky fog of her consciousness, a voice interrupted her typing.

"Ma'am? Another whiskey and soda?"

Swinging her head to the sound, Barbara let a silly smile light her face. The woman already had the drink in hand. She nodded, and dug more bills from her purse. Sipping at the beverage, she finished the message and sent it.

BT: 'Batteries are running low, both figuratively and literally. I've got my whiskey and soda, but no way to charge up my phone. See you when I get home. Feel better, baby.'

She waited, watching the icon spin. Barbara read his last message before she darkened the lighted screen and placed the device in her purse.

ST: 'Can't wait to see you. Love you lots.'

The seat didn't go back very far, but she reclined it as much as possible. Whether it was the warm flush of her skin, or the cold prickles that kept clinging to her spine, or all the whiskey she couldn't remember drinking, she suddenly was having trouble keeping her eyes open. The spinning nausea almost stopped altogether when she closed her eyes, and she only opened them long enough to take another sip of her drink.

Barbara frowned; it was empty again. She shook her head, closed her eyes and drifted off.

* * *

Barbara woke to the sound of the captain announcing that they would be descending shortly. She was still swathed in a thick haze of clinging confusion, or unconsciousness. After punching at the button on her phone a half dozen times and still not seeing the light, she realized that the battery had been completely exhausted. It was the same way Barbara felt, although she had slept a good many hours on the flight. She stared at the empty drink in front of her dully until the flight attendant came to collect it, and tell her that all seats needed to be fully upright and all trays stowed for landing. Barbara followed the commands dully, slowly, mindlessly.

Nearly forgetting her carry-on, then her purse, Barbara still felt as thought she were leaving something valuable behind. She patted at her pockets and clothes; everywhere except her belly, where a peculiar tingling made it tender to the touch. The thoughts in her head were tenuous strands of disconnected meaninglessness. Nothing but dense wet fog filled her head, and her mental landscape was wordless static. Shuffling out between all the other people shuffling out,

Barbara followed the thickest stream of them to baggage claim. She fell behind, her steps slowing to a struggled stagger as she approached the trundling cycle.

She couldn't remember why she was there after a minute. Looking around, she spotted the woman that had been coughing next to her on the flight. It was like spotting a familiar feature in an alien landscape, seeing a glimpse of remembered reality in a senseless dream. Barbara couldn't say why, but for some reason she began to move towards the woman. Her shuffled steps were slow pained movements, and the woman was intercepted by two other people before Barbara could get close. She stood there, watching them interact, shaking with anger or hunger or weakness.

They led the woman away, and Barbara cocked her head curiously to watch them. It was not her friends, or family; it was a man and woman, stiff and in suits. Although they were not handling her physically, it was clear that they had taken her into some sort of custody. They flanked her, watching the frail lady like she may attack them at any moment. Barbara heard a low moan escape her own lips, some part of the feelings she couldn't identify within dripping out her slack jaw to find expression in the world. Her eyes went to the rolling luggage track, trying to remember what it was and why it was moving. A part of her screamed at her to get away, to run; her mind quivered like her weak legs, past making sense of anything.

Passengers got their bags, one by one, and began to disperse. Barbara stood there through it all, trembling and hesitating interminably. There were only a few people left waiting for their bags when the pair in suits returned. They walked towards her, watching her as they approached. That unidentifiable fear within her rose up again, and Barbara's hand went to her tender belly. She moaned, in pained uncertainty.

"Ma'am?" The woman stopped before her. "Could we have a word please?"

They stood a few feet from each other, as if blocking her escape. Barbara knew that if she tried to run, it would only end in her sprawled at their feet. She didn't have the mental power required to envision herself staggering slowly away from them, or to laugh at the image of them chasing her at an easy walking pace. One single thought came into her mind, and she tried to express it verbally as she dug in her purse for her phone. She stabbed at the power button repeatedly, moaning the single word again and again. Each time it sounded less like a word and more like an animal: eating, or dying, or both.

"Stanley," she moaned. "Shanley. Sanny. Saargh…"

Barbara dropped her phone, then fell to her knees. They made a thick squishing sound as they struck the hard floor. Coming up beside her, the agents approached cautiously. For some reason she thought of biting one of them; it seemed the only clear thought that she had formed in some time. Her movements were too thick and slow and syrupy to catch one of them; Barbara felt them haul her to her feet by her elbows. She fought, or tried to, as they began coaxing her away from her fallen phone.

The man sent her sprawling, and Barbara fell too fast to get her hands under her. She cracked her chin on the floor. The tip of her tongue was severed by the blow, and a tiny lump of bloody pink flesh landed between her and her phone. Barbara lurched forward, taking the meat in her mouth and swallowing it as she reached for her phone. Her wrists were pulled behind her, one and then the other, and cuffed together.

"She's strong," the woman said.

They helped her to her feet once more. Each of them held her by an elbow, and started walking. Barbara watched her phone until she couldn't crane her neck to see it any more, then hung her bruised chin to her chest.

"She'll keep getting stronger," the man nodded. "When the first change takes hold."

The woman looked at Barbara, like she was some kind of curious specimen; she cocked her head to one side, then addressed the man as if Barbara wasn't there once again.

"Have you seen this before?" she asked. "People getting infected without being bitten?"

"No," the man replied calmly. "I don't know what to make of it. They must have been ill already, with seriously compromised immune systems."

Barbara looked back and forth between them; she tried to form a word, or a thought. Instead she stumbled, and moaned.

"Are we taking her back to base?" The woman looked disgusted by the thought.

"No." The man shook his head. "We'll take her to the hospital."

"What about the other woman?"

He nodded. "We'll take her too. Call

County. Tell them to be ready for two outbreak victims."

The woman threw a sidelong glance at Barbara. She shuddered. "Can't we just take them to General South? It's closer."

"They don't have proper quarantine facilities." The man almost smiled. "Don't worry. You won't catch it. They only caught it because they were already sick. I'm sure of it."

* * *

Barbara could only see enough through the plastic partitions to know there was someone in the next room. She could only hear enough to know that people were nearby, somewhere; they stayed away from her room. Her hands were restrained, and she could only reach far enough to lift the scrap of thin hospital gown to look at her belly. It was a twisted network of bloodied tissue, spiraling outward from her umbilical center to claim more healthy skin with each passing hour. Barbara had seen burn scars before, and that's what it reminded her of; red and yellow and clear fluids gathered in the pitted exposed sinew, and glistened on the high fleshy ridges. Somehow the tip of her tongue had grown back, but everything else felt like it was sagging at the seams.

Drifting in and out of consciousness, Barbara had no way to tell how much time was passing. There were clocks on the walls, and a television on in the next room; somehow printed numbers and spoken words were all nonsensical images and meaningless noises to her fogged brain. There were no windows to tell if it was day or night, and both passed as she lay there waiting. She had forgotten what she was waiting for, or if she had ever known. The hunger twisting at her belly felt as though it was consuming every last part of who she used to be; no one brought her food, although that wasn't what she hungered for. Her thoughts dwindled to nothing, her memories slipped away, and her belly continued to reach long tendrils of rot further across her torso.

Only one thought remained to her, and it wasn't even really a thought. It was a word, a single word that rolled around in her mouth and echoed in the hollow chambers of her mind. Sometimes she would say it out loud, or try to, just to hear it fall on her own ears. Most of those times it was more of a growl or a moan than a word, but every now and then she got it right. When she did, a silly mindless smile would break out across her ashen face; several minutes might pass then before she fiddled with the growing wound on her torso.

"Stanley." Barbara said it, almost perfectly, and smiled. She covered her belly with the thin hospital gown, stared at the white ceiling. A moment later two figures entered the room, and she stared at them, confused. Some part of her had expected to waste away in this room, passing into whatever waited beyond the sheets of plastic and the curtain of death without ever seeing another living being. Another part of her had been obsessed with that single thought, that one word that kept her anchored in this world. All of the other parts of her had been ravaged like the smooth skin that once had covered her slim belly; it was too much for her to recognize the man and woman standing over her in dark suits.

The woman was looking down at her, her face twisted in revulsion.

"She looks worse than the other one," she said. "You can barely tell she's the same woman we brought in here a couple days ago."

"She's not," the man said. He looked like he felt bad for Barbara. "Be careful. It looks like the change has taken hold almost completely."

"She doesn't look as bad as the girl back at base, though," the woman noted. "What was her name?"

"Elayna," the man answered. "She's different. We've never seen it take hold like that. It's always something that starts from the inside, whether the victim is bitten or whether they are vulnerable due to a compromised immune system. That one...it's like it started from the outside and worked its way in. The symptoms that usually happen last happened immediately with her; the precursors only showed up after we had taken her into custody. It's curious."

She looked at him, narrowed her eyes.

"How long have you been studying these things?" she asked.

He shook his head.

"You know I can't talk about that," he said, shaking his head. He looked at Barbara. "Especially in front of her."

The woman laughed bitterly. She waved her hand in front of Barbara's face. Barbara laid there, her eyes tracking the movement while her body stayed rigid, stiff and still.

"Her?" The woman laughed. "She is clearly beyond communicating, or comprehending."

"Don't be so sure," the man cautioned her. "If we administer the cure it will all come back to her, perhaps even this conversation."

The woman moved her hand away just as Barbara lunged forward at it. The movement looked more like a shift than a lunge from the outside; they barely noticed.

"What if she feeds?" The woman asked. A fresh wave of revulsion crossed her face.

"It will all come back to her then too," he sighed. "It will be viewed from a different perspective, but she will be aware of it."

The woman shuddered. "Then why keep feeding?"

He shrugged, chuckled. "Most of us in this country look like horrible monsters to chickens and cows and pigs. We raise them in horrific conditions that the government won't allow us to see, lest we realize what monsters we really are when we order a chicken sandwich or a hamburger from McBurger Queen."

She shuddered again. "Not me. I'm a vegetarian."

"Oh, come on." He nudged her playfully. "You must realize that all kinds of wildlife are misplaced or killed by farming those vegetables. Besides, when did fruits and vegetables fall off everyone's list of living, breathing, feeling things? Science shows that a plant reacts with alarm when we attack it, or even other plants near it. So you're not a monster to animals, maybe, if you source all your seed stock from sustainable organic farms and grow most of your own food. You're still a homicidal maniac in your garden, deciding who lives and who dies based on what you feel hungry for. It's all a matter of perspective. If I were a tomato I would see you as the most terrifying monster on the planet. I would rather ripen and rot on the vine than be picked and eaten at my prime, no matter what life form I happen to be. Wouldn't you?"

The woman laughed. "Why do I even bother arguing with you?"

"I don't know," the man shrugged. "I wonder about that too."

Before she could smile, or speak, a scream sounded in the hallway. It was followed by another, then a chorus of them. The next sound was like nothing she had ever heard; it was a howl and a screech and a word all at the same time. It was as if an animal with a mouth full of teeth and tongue were calling out a name. Barbara couldn't wrap her head around the conversation between them, but she knew that name. It was her name.

"Barbara!"

She sat up, and was surprised when her restraints tore easily. The man and the woman both had their backs to her, and it looked as though they had drawn weapons.

Barbara cried out, the only word she knew, the word she had practiced so diligently as she had wasted away. The only improvement in her condition had been the only one she needed, her tongue growing back as the rest of her had dwindled to mindless hunger. She used it now, to call to him.

"Stanley!"

She watched the suited pair turn, look at her and move away. Barbara heard another scream in the hallway. She cried out again.

"Stanley!"

They stared at the door, the three of them, hearts pounding for different reasons. Barbara reached down, tore the thick fabric of her leg restraints from their moorings, sat on the edge of the bed, and waited.

ABOUT STAN'S SNIFFLES

That was exciting, right? And fun, hopefully. If you liked the man and woman that took the two ladies into custody, look forward to learning more about them in upcoming short stories. They're also in the book, but you wouldn't know it by looking at them.

If you want to make sure all those blanks get filled in, you'll want to pick up volume four of the short story collections. It is called 'The Zombie Killers'.

Right now, it's time for the final story in this set. It's called 'Stan's Sniffles', and it's about Barbara's husband. It's also about the way things are going down out there in the world, and how the ramblers and howlers are hitting the streets at last.

Stan is a pretty great guy. He's keeping a secret, but it's not out of any malevolent intentions. You'll find out that secret soon, and see how some secrets can't be kept when the monster comes to call.

We each need to be ferocious in some way, if we expect to be or do what we want.

Just as there is both strength and weakness in kindness, and just as they vary in every instance, so is there both strength and weakness in hearing nothing but one's hunger. The heart hungers, as does the soul; in polite society, those are the only howls we hear. But those parts of us only have the strength to cry out if an individual's basic needs are met. What is it like, to have your whole consciousness twisted by a hunger for flesh? I had to know, and I had to like the person whose rusted red eyes I was looking through.

That person was Stan. You heard him howling in the end of the last story; let's see how he found Barbara, and what happens after he does. As always, I hope you enjoy reading it as much as I loved writing it.

This story was the seventh one that I got started on. When I saw how lean and clean and ferocious it wanted to be, I got all excited and finished it fourth. I did go in some kind of order on these, as you'll see over time; this set was one that I jumped back and forth between stories on, starting all three before finishing any of them. Stan's story was the first one completed; you'll soon see why I chose to make it the finale in the set.

STAN'S SNIFFLES

Reading the last message on the lighted screen in his hand, Stanley sniffled and coughed and frowned all at the same time. His gaze roamed the scattered mess that was the living room. It looked like a disaster area, a concentric ring of castoffs from the last week covering the carpet around the sofa. He darkened the screen, picked up the television remote. He turned the volume up on the game and snagged a tissue from the dwindling box. Blowing his nose loudly, he spoke aloud.

"Barbara," he said, sniffling. "I'm dying."

He shook his head, tried again.

"Sweetheart, I have something to tell you." Stanley coughed up a mouthful of phlegm, spit it in the tissue and tossed it on the pile. It drifted past spent bottles of cough syrup and wrappers torn from chocolate covered granola bars to land amidst a small mountain of similarly crumpled and stained sheets of softness.

"You know how I said I had the flu?" he continued. "Well, that was only half of the truth. The doctor actually said that I have flu-like symptoms caused by...well, it's caused by tuberculosis. Barbara, honey, I have TB."

Stanley watched the game more intently for the space of a minute, leaning forward in his pile of sweaty blankets. His robe stuck to his back, warm and wet.

"Oh, come on!" he shouted at the screen. "That was clearly a foul. Where's the damned flag? Where's the damned flag?!"

Settling back into the softness of the cushions and blankets, his face become grave once more. He spoke again, staring off at nothing.

"No, sweetie, not that kind of tuberculosis. I have multi-drug resistant tuberculosis. It's a sleek modern version of the ancient killer. Those of us in the know call it 'MDR TB', since we know we don't have much time left. No, Barbie, they can't cure it; that's why it's called-"

Stanley lurched forward, nearly toppling forward onto the littered mess. He made obscene hand gestures, and shouted some more.

"Home field advantage doesn't mean you only call fouls on the visitors! This is ridiculous! It's not even subtle!"

He heard an alert from the otherwise

inert device. Lifting it from the coffee table, Stanley pressed a single button and tapped the lighted screen. A message had appeared under the thread of their last exchange.

BT: 'Batteries are running low, both figuratively and literally. I've got my whiskey and soda, but no way to charge up my phone. See you when I get home. Feel better, baby.'

He typed up a quick response, set the device back on the coffee table, and returned to his slow shameless deterioration. Stanley let his hand hover over the cluttered surface for a moment; he selected two items, and fell back into the sofa. Sipping at the scotch, he read the labels plastered about the tiny bottle for the hundredth time. One of them said that he shouldn't be drinking; but that was just unreasonable. The other said to take one every four hours; that was reasonable enough, unless he managed to sleep eight hours. What was he supposed to do then, take two? It hadn't happened yet, so he hadn't researched it.

The other label said he needed to take it with food. There was a nondescript black and white rendition of a sandwich next to the warning; just looking at it made his stomach turn. The thought of getting up to make an actual sandwich made him break out into a cold sweat, and Stanley chased the taste of bile from his mouth with more scotch. Leaning forward once more, he seized the box of salted crackers from the coffee table. He knocked over a bottle of cough syrup, and made no move to right it. Stanley nibbled on a single cracker, tossed half of it to the floor uneaten, took the pill with a generous helping of whiskey, and cuddled deeper into the giant mountain of blankets.

* * *

Stanley woke up a few hours later, in a drugged and drunken stupor. He had spilt both crackers and scotch on himself in his sleep, and he couldn't seem to read the clock on the cable box. He shut off the television; it was still blaring, some other game that just looked like blurred moving colors to him. The sudden silence startled him, and he turned it back on, put on some cartoons at a lower volume. He took another pill, drank the rest of the whiskey, and curled up even tighter in the cocoon of blankets. Sliding in and out of consciousness, deep in the grips of fever and pain and deterioration, Stanley had no idea that time was passing as it was.

Of course there were moments when he

wondered if she should have been home by now, if something had happened; or if he needed to get the place cleaned up. He also wondered if he was taking too many pills, or too few; and if the strange twisted mound of tenderness on his belly was really there or not. Stanley knew that the little winged lights and horned devils dancing around his head were definitely not real, but everything else was up for debate. After what seemed minutes or months, depending on how he looked at it, Stanley finally roused himself to have a look in the mirror and maybe wash some of what had actually been three days off of himself in the shower.

His fever had broken, and the ache in his belly had turned to a strange twisting hunger. Stanley had seriously considered that he would die without ever knowing the sweet sharp pang of hunger again, that he would never eat another meal without it being tasteless and uninteresting. Now it gnawed at him, and pulled what little energy he had left from his very bones to feed it. Stanley staggered to the bathroom, his outstretched hand on the wall for support as he ambled slowly up the hallway. Twice he stumbled, fell to his knees, and sat that way for a full minute. He listened to the slow tortured rattle of his own labored breathing, gathering his strength to stand both times. Finally he made it to the bathroom, flipped on the overhead, and blinked in the light.

Stanley stepped back, cried out. The step was a stumble, the cry an anguished growl. He looked in the mirror, staring at every change that had taken place on the parts of his body that he could see. His hands and face were gray, the skin turned dry and translucent. As he watched, a flaky hunk of flesh fell from his face to the tiled floor. Stanley cried out again; once more it was an unfamiliar sound. His voice was that of a hungry or tormented animal. He let the thought come to him that this was another fevered hallucination, or some unforeseen stage of his disease; then he let the reality of his monstrosity sink in.

Meeting his own eyes in the mirror, rusted red locked on rusted red; Stanley growled his surprise, and his hunger, as his other cheek fell at his feet. He let his robe fall away, and saw the creature in the mirror stand there staring at him in a pair of his own boxer shorts. The creature moved when he did, opened its toothy maw when he did, growled when he did. Stanley let his last effort at coherent thought fall away like his robe had a minute earlier. Ambling to the door, still in his boxers, he fumbled at the locks for several minutes before his hand turned the knob. He stepped into the hallway.

"Stanley!" His neighbor from across the hall called out to him, standing guarded in his own door jamb. "I had no idea you were in there. Are you alright? Have you been watching the news? There's some kind of outbreak. Some people are saying that it's zombies..."

The man stopped talking as Stanley swung his head around slowly. He sniffed at the air while his neighbor's face went white, and his trembling voice trailed off. Purposefully, Stanley turned and began moving toward him. The man slammed the door shut, and the sound of a half dozen locks being engaged clicked and clacked loudly while Stanley dragged his hunger down the hallway. He could hear shouting from the other side of the door; he could smell fear, and flesh. It took him awhile to reach the door; once he did, it splintered under his slow unyielding fingers. Stanley burst through the wooden barrier in twitching hungry stops and starts.

He went for the little one; not out of

logic or fear or decisiveness, but out of simple savage hunger. Stanley was no longer Stanley; the hunger that twisted at his belly had wrung him dry of every other aspect of his experience, and he went for the baby even as her parents came up behind him. His belly full for a brief moment, he turned from the ravaged little corpse as the next change began to come over him. Stanley's twitching slow movement became a wild predator's rapid charge as his belly turned flesh to power.

Biting him, and then her, Stanley alternated between them until they stopped fighting him off. When their arms opened to embrace him, he rolled away and let the rest of the change wash over him. Rows of jagged teeth sprouted in his mouth, pushing the dull old ones out. The way his arms and legs grew longer and more defined was painful; Stanley leapt to his new legs, cried out his pain and his hunger. The couple came at him, to feed him; Stanley pushed them away with his powerful new talons. He leapt through their window, howling his hunger at the night as he fell.

Hitting the pavement several stories below, Stanley's legs absorbed the impact like steel springs. He leapt again, using the momentum of the fall to bounce forward over a streetlight and several automobiles. Running was faster, so that's what he did; he outran cars on all but the most speedy freeways, tearing a passenger through their window as he passed when the hunger twisted at his belly. It was quicker than he could have imagined a trip to the hospital before; in less than twenty minutes time, and a few blurred bites of pedestrians for fuel, Stanley burst into the emergency room. He howled, watching the people waiting in chairs draw back, or scream.

Stanley sniffed the air. Although the part of his face that used to be his nose was just two narrow open cavities at this point, his sense of smell was beyond compare. It was like flipping through the facility's most secret files in a series of whiffs. There were the dead, starting to awaken in the basement; there were the dying, beginning to turn and smelling nothing like food; and there were the living, inviting him hungrily up hallways full of folks in casts and waiting rooms and break rooms throughout the hospital. For another moment he sniffed, just to make sure; then he grasped a man from his seat, tossed him over his shoulder, and ran.

Nibbling on the man's leg, Stanley felt

his snack stop fighting him and start pressing his own flesh at into the jagged rows of his monstrous teeth. Running, eating, bouncing the meat along on his shoulder, Stanley had mostly finished him by the time he reached the next emergency room. He burst through the sliding glass before it could move aside, still holding the man's stripped skull in his grip. A dozen people began screaming at once, and Stanley howled at them so they might shut up. He lifted the ragged remains of his nose to the air, sniffed.

Stanley rose to his full fearful height, and howled. He tore a young woman's arm off as he smashed through the next pane of glass. Gnawing on it, Stanley lifted his nose to the air. He dropped the arm, clutched the skull to his torso, and ran up the hallway. Skidding past a closed door, he retraced his steps and went through it. In the stairwell, he sniffed at the air, above and below. He leapt up one flight of stairs after the other, to burst through another door and sniff at the air. Stanley collected his thoughts, filled his lungs, and cried out as intelligibly as he could.

"Barbara!"

It was the first word he had tried to form since before the first change had come over him. It was technically not even really a word; it was more of a growl or a howl, something like a mix between an animal being eaten and the animal that was eating it. He was shocked to hear a strangled response.

"Stanley?"

Her voice sounded twisted as well; lower, and more guttural. It echoed down the hall like his had, the tortured strangled words falling on what used to be his ears like sweet music.

"Stanley?!"

Faster than he could think, Stanley moved. He tore down the hallway, through plastic curtains, past every fragile piece of reality that stood between them. People and their parts rose behind him like the wake of a speedboat when they got in his way, and a wet slick trail of fat red droplets followed him into the wide open space. Machines beeped and whirred, masked hospital staff fled in every direction; and for a moment he stood on the tiled floor and simply stared at her.

Bullets tore into him, from one side and from behind. Stanley ignored the annoying pricks of pain, except to angle himself between the flying lead and the object of his desire. Moving toward her, he smiled as she lifted her hospital gown to show him her belly. It was a twisted mess of rotting flesh, visible sinew and exposed veins. He smiled, showing her his endless rows of teeth, and held the skull he still carried between them. Tilting forward slowly, she clacked her teeth against the dead face ineffectively.

Stanley pulled the skull away from her, gently, dropped it on the tiled floor and stepped on it. A series of quiet popping sounds ended in one loud satisfying crack, and he bent to retrieve the rotting ball of flesh. Holding it out to her again, Stanley let his smile broaden as he watched her dig at the wide crack. He watched her begin to change, the top of her skull losing the few loose clumps of remaining hair as it grew thicker and denser. When she had sucked the bony container dry, she looked up and smiled back at him. Their rusted eyes met, and he saw the hunger in hers.

Turning, not looking back, Stanley exploded from the room and skidded into the hallway. More bullets came at him, and he raised himself to his full height and howled at his attackers. A man and woman stood side by side, dressed nearly identically in pressed black on starched white. They were fearless, shoulder to shoulder as they emptied clips into him. The only time their hands moved was to drop a clip to the floor and slam another home, chamber a round and begin firing once more. Stanley grabbed a row of chairs, tore them from their moorings and tossed them at the annoying pair. The man put his body between the woman and the chairs as they came at them; they went down in a twisted pile of limbs and broken seats.

He didn't have to look back to see if she followed; he heard her, felt her, sensed her. Stanley felt her thoughts clearer than the words her toothy mouth could no longer form, heard her hunger crying out to her irresistibly. He grabbed a nurse and threw him to the floor, holding him until her hunger was slaked. Leaving the stripped mess of bones in the wet puddle of blood that had formed as she fed, Stanley dashed up the length of the hallway. He felt her behind him as he ran, as he burst through the window, and as he fell to the street below. They landed side by side, on their feet.

The sun was gone, dropped over the horizon. The last few rays of light lit the rooftops and plunged alleys into inky darkness. Through his rusted red eyes, Stanley saw heat signatures all over the city;

he heard frightened heartbeats for miles, and it sounded like a sweet chorus of melodious dinner bells ringing in his monstrous ears. Lifting the exposed gashes that were his nose, Stanley sniffed and smiled. He began walking, slowly, letting the power in his limbs build as the hunger twisted at his belly.

She moved silently, slightly faster than him, moving to catch up and match his pace. Neither of them spoke, or tried to, although a monstrous growl slipped from one of them from time to time. The smell grew stronger and the heat signature came clearer as the outer wall drew closer. Before bursting through the layers of thin materials between him and their dinner, Stanley paused. He felt her thoughts, her presence, her hunger. He turned to her, extended one taloned hand to the monster that his wife had become. She took it, held it, squeezed it, and let go.

Turning suddenly, Barbara howled and attacked the barrier. Chips of paint and splinters of wood rained on Stanley as he watched, and a wide toothy smile stretched across the twisted thing that used to be his face. He raised himself to his full height and howled, singing his response to the screeching call of the woman on the other side of the wall. He watched Barbara tear through insulation and studs to grasp the screaming woman. He watched his wife take the first bite, the second, the third; there was no pause between, nothing but primal hunger and animalistic speed as she tore the woman's shoulder to pulsing hamburger.

Stanley felt a trickle of moisture on his fleshless cheek; he lifted a clawed finger to wipe it away; the tear was red and warm, a single drop of blood. He howled, burst through the wall and took the woman to the ground. They gorged on her, together, until every last bit of flesh had been stripped from her bones. There was a closeness there that they had never felt before, a connection that brought them together more completely than ever; when they were done, they scoured the city for fresh flesh, dining at all of the establishments they had been unable to afford in their previous life together. In between kills, they linked their clawed fingers together and walked the empty streets. When a howl would sound somewhere in the city, they would drop their hands and howl together, as thousands of hungered cries filled the night sky.

It wasn't life, or like any version of it they had imagined together; but it wasn't death either, knocking at the door and clawing at the windows all at once. It was just Stanley and Barbara, together again, chasing a hunger that would never stop gnawing at them. It was, in many ways, the closest they had ever been.

Dear Reader,

I hope you loved the stories, and don't tire of hearing me say so. It's a special thing to have a story speak to me, and to get to know it's characters over time. Equally special is the relationship between author and reader, and the opportunity for us to get to know each other better. I can be a weird guy; I know that, and I embrace it. My writing spans many genres, and not all of it is for everyone. That's why there is plenty of sample stuff on my website, and lots of free quality content for newsletter subscribers.

This year the content is largely these short stories, along with secret weekly messages and secret giveaways. If you liked these stories, I encourage you to sign up for the newsletter. It's free to join, and you'll become a secret member of the 'Secret Society of Deeper Meaning'. Next year we'll be...oh yeah, it's a secret.

As far as getting to know you, we are adding more live book festivals to our calendar every year. Check the websites, JayNorry.com or SuddenInsightPublishing. com, to find out when we'll be near you.

If we're not coming close enough, let us know about a festival in your area and we'll see about making it out. There are few things more gratifying to me than meeting someone who loves my books, or thinks they might. I adore my blood relatives, but my intellectual family are the ones I really go the extra mile for.

If you're the kind of reader I used to be, getting out and going to book festivals might not rouse you. That's fine; send me a message, if you want to let me know what you think. I'm a busy guy, so it might take a little while; but I'll get back to you.

Also, reader reviews are very important to independent authors; even a star rating and a few simple words can help a book better find its ideal reader. I would truly appreciate you taking the time to review this on Amazon and/or Goodreads. If you want help, I wrote a guide for writing book reviews that is located on that website I keep talking about. Thanks for reading!

All the best,

Jay

Jay@JayNorry.com

Twitter: @JayNorry

www.ingramcontent.com/pod-product-compliance
Lightning Source LLC
Chambersburg PA
CBHW051712180726

48283CB00004B/1311